Stories from

Junior Readers Series

1. *The Drum* — Chinua Achebe
2. *Adventure in Nakuru* — Juma Bustani
3. *The Poor Child* — David Maillu
4. *Growing up at Lina School* — Oludhe Macgoye
5. *Adventure in Mombasa* — Juma Bustani
6. *Kisalu and His Fruit Garden and Other Stories* — David Maillu
7. *The Motherless Baby* — Cyprian Ekwensi
8. *Adventure in Nairobi* — Juma Bustani
9. *The Smugglers* — Barbara Kimenye
10. *Chike and the River* — Chinua Achebe
11. *Yasin in Trouble* — Martha Mvungi
12. *The Great Elephant Bird* — Cyprian Ekwensi
13. *The Boa Suitor* — Cyprian Ekwensi
14. *Moses and the Man from Mars* — Barbara Kimenye
15. *The Drummer Boy* — Cyprian Ekwensi
16. *East African Why Stories* — Pamela Kola
17. *East African When Stories* — Pamela Kola
18. *East African How Stories* — Pamela Kola
19. *The Scoop* — Barbara Kimenye
20. *The Gemstone Affair* — Barbara Kimenye
21. *The Cunning Tortoise* — Pamela Kola
22. *Ogilo and the Hippo* — Asenath Odaga
23. *Moses in a Mess* — Barbara Kimenye
24. *Stories from a Shona Childhood* — Charles Mungoshi
25. *Tales of the Secret Valley* — Tim Mathews
26. *Sing Me a Song* — (ed) Leteipa Ole Sunkuli
27. *Why the Cat Lives with People* — Margaret Okello
28. *Shaka Zulu* — Jonti Marks
29. *The Snake with Seven Heads* — Gcina Mhlophe
30. *Queen of the Tortoises* — Gcina Mhlophe
31. *The Calabash Child* — Diana Pitcher
32. *One Day Long Ago* — Charles Mungoshi
33. *The Priceless Gift* — David Maillu
34. *The Singing Dog* — Gcina Mhlophe
35. *A Girl Who Could Not Keep Quiet* — Rose Mwagi
36. *Adventures of Pongo and Uncle Talema* — George G.N. Kamau
37. *Bonolo and the Peach Tree* — Njabulo Ndebele
38. *Misa, the Precious Cow* — Jimmi Makotsi .
39. *Tales of Tortoise and Lion* — Henry Enahoro
40. *Kobole's Misfortunes* — Athman Amran
41. *Stories from Uganda* — James Appe
42. *More Stories from Uganda* — James Appe
43. *Njamba Nene and the Flying Bus* — Ngugi wa Thiong'o

Are you a primary school boy or girl? How many of these books have you read? You will improve both your written and spoken English greatly each time you read a book in this series. Besides, you will find the stories very interesting. Try to read as many of these books as possible. You should even make it a point to read each book several times.

EDITOR

Junior Readers Series 41

Stories from Uganda

James Appe

East African Educational Publishers
Nairobi

Published by
East African Educational Publishers Ltd.
Brick Court
Mpaka Road/Woodvale Grove
Westlands
P.O. Box 45314, Nairobi

© James Appe, 1994
First published 1994

ISBN 9966 - 46 - 727 - 0

Typeset by
Views Media
Ngong Road, off Kindaruma Lane
P.O. Box 50041, Nairobi

Printed by
Printpak
Likoni Road
P.O. Box 78354
Nairobi, Kenya

Lion and His Wives

Lion had many wives. He had fifteen wives at one time but most of them soon ran away because he was an insatiable husband in every way. They were also afraid of his cruelty, bad temper and greed.

But some of the wives, like Monkey, left because Lion found them lazy and too insolent. So in the end he was left with only five wives — Frog, Scorpion, Snake, Grasshopper and Crab.

Frog was the favourite wife. She always received the fattest meat that Lion brought from his daily hunting. She, alone, was allowed to be present when Lion received visitors. Then Lion liked Frog, then Scorpion, then Snake, and Grasshopper. Lion liked Crab the least, and gave her bony meat such as the horns and hoofs of animals.

But Lion did not know that Crab was the one who loved him the most. In fact if it was not for her, the other wives would have killed Lion within a short time. But Crab was a good wife who never complained about the way her husband treated her, nor did she tell him about the dreadful plots against him by the other wives. The only thing she did was to prevent the other wives from killing Lion because she loved him so much. This is how the plot against Lion was carried out.

Every day, at about midday, when Frog knew Lion was deep in the forests on his hunting trips, she would come out of her house and sit in the sun for sometime, praying for evil to fall upon the husband she hated. She was a magician and could bring rain even in the dry season. When she began to sweat in the heat of the sun, Frog would lift up her eyes, and look at the sun until the tears, gathered in her eyes, conjured up rain clouds from all the corners of the sky. When the clouds became very black and roared, Frog would let her tears drop on the ground. At once it would begin to rain. Frog would croak once or twice,

then run back into her house, praying that the rain should kill Lion in the forests.

It was the custom that every wife must do all she can to save her husband's life whenever he was in danger. So, as soon as it began to pour, Frog, as the senior wife, would come out and pretend to stop the rain. She would croak once or twice, then go back into her house. Scorpion would come out next and perform some rituals, and she too would retreat. Snake and Grasshopper would also do the same. But these four wives were more concerned about themselves than they were about their husband's well-being.

Crab, however, always tried all she could to stop the rain. With her voice full of pity, she cried and beat the ground with her head as she sang.

> Oh sky, oh sky!
> Please open up for me
> The Lion is my only husband
> Please open up for me!

Crab prayed like this and pleaded with the sky until the rain stopped. For many years things went on like this, and it looked as if Lion would never notice.

One day an old woman who lived nearby came to Lion and tried to tell him the truth about his wives. Lion refused to listen. He was not going to allow anyone to spoil the relationship with his wives, he said. But in the end the woman got Lion to agree to see things for himself.

The next day, Lion did not go far on his hunting trip. He killed a young antelope near his home and then climbed up a tall tree from where he could see his compound.

As usual, Frog got out of her house at midday and invoked the rain with her magic. The entire drama was repeated in front of Lion's eyes. He was so enraged that it was difficult for him to wait for Crab to end the rain. So as soon as the rain abated Lion rushed home and made straight for Frog's house. He held her by the neck and pushed her to the floor with such force that

Frog's eyes flew out of her head. Lion crushed her under his feet and hurried to the houses of Scorpion and Snake. He killed both of them in the same way. Only Grasshopper and Crab were left as his wives now.

So, in the end, Crab became Lion's favourite wife. He transferred all the fat meat from Frog's house to Crab's. And Lion lived happily ever after with his two loving wives.

Hare and Kenyi

Hare and Kenyi were brothers. The two lived in the same compound, but they were different in every way. Kenyi was patient and humble, while Hare was arrogant and bad-mannered. Whereas Kenyi was a successful farmer, Hare was a hunter.

There was a long drought and plants died in the farms leading to widespread famine everywhere. People began eating the little food they had stored behind closed doors lest a poor neighbour should want to share it. Those who had cows lived on milk. Those who had no animals had nothing to eat.

Now Hare had tamed a group of baboons whom he milked everyday. He dipped his millet bread in the milk and ate it, but refused to give his brother Kenyi any milk. When he found Kenyi's millet bread in his milk, he threw it or fed it to his baboons. Kenyi begged his brother to be understanding, but Hare refused to listen.

Kenyi could not bear this any longer. So one day he set out for a distant kingdom, intending to pawn himself to the king in return for at least one cow so that he would have milk to dip his millet bread in. He walked and walked for many months, living on wild roots. When at last he arrived at the king's palace, he was too ashamed to go through the gate. So he sat on the rubbish heap outside, eating the left overs that had been thrown there.

In the late afternoon, one of the king's cocks came by. When the cock saw Kenyi, it began to throw rubbish on him.

But Kenyi sat quietly and humbly, not daring even to wipe the dirt on his face. Then one of the king's wives came and threw more rubbish on Kenyi. But Kenyi looked down all the time and did not complain. Then suddenly the cock cried out in a loud voice: "Oh King! This visitor of yours here is a good man. Come and take him home."

The king replied: "If he is a good man, bring him inside!"

Kenyi was immediately taken inside the palace and put in one of the visitor's rooms. He sat under a large structure to await his orders. The same cock came and got on the structure. It threw down delicious foods — meat, honey and sweet fruits. But Kenyi did not touch anything. He did not even lick the honey that got on his hands. Again the cock cried out: "Oh King! Oh King! This visitor of yours here is a good man. Come and take him away from here." And the king replied: "If he is a good man, bring him here to me."

Kenyi was taken to the king and asked to speak out. When he told the king why he had come to his kingdom, he ordered food for him and then he went to sleep.

The following day Kenyi was given a gourd full of cowpea seeds and asked to go to the farm to sow it. He agreed and worked until late in the afternoon when he finished sowing the seeds. But when he got back to the palace, the king exclaimed: "What! Have you finished sowing all the seeds in the farm in such a short time? I do not believe it! It takes five people to finish that amount of seed in such a short time. You must have eaten the seeds. Go back and pick out every seed so I can see if you have not eaten them!"

Kenyi was very miserable and hungry, but obeyed the king at once. He collected hundreds of doves and asked them to help him collect the seeds.

"My friends," he pleaded with them, "please do not swallow a single seed even if a seed goes down your throat. Spit it out and bring it to me." The doves were obedient and did not eat a single seed. They picked up all the seeds and Kenyi brought them to the king.

"I believe you now", the king announced when he saw the retrieved seed, "you are a good man. Now go back and sow the seeds again." Kenyi went and did as he was ordered, and then came back home.

Kenyi worked for the king for three months then asked to be allowed to return to his country. The king gave him hundreds of cows and bulls and goats. Kenyi drove his herd home very slowly, allowing the animals to eat on the way. It took him almost six months. All the cows gave birth on the way so by the time he reached his own country, the number of his animals had more than doubled.

Hare had just finished milking his baboons when someone told him Kenyi was coming back with many cattle. At first he was not much interested, but eventually he went and climbed a tall tree behind his house. Sure enough, in the distance he saw a sea of cattle moving slowly towards their home. He climbed down hurriedly and made for his herd of baboons.

"Go away, you miserable creatures!" he shouted at them. "Are you not ashamed to stay here when my brother is bringing thousands of REAL COWS! Off you go! Back to the bush where you belong." He rushed to get his spear and it was only by a quick dash around the house that the baboons saved themselves.

But alas! Kenyi completely refused to give Hare a drop of milk. He gave his surplus milk to the neighbours, but not to Hare.

Hare could not bear this humiliation any longer, and so he also set out for the distant kingdom, intending to pawn himself as Kenyi had done.

After walking for many months, he finally arrived at the king's palace. He stood at the gate and proudly announced himself. A servant ordered him to sit on the rubbish heap and wait there. While he was waiting, the cock came and started throwing rubbish on him.

"What!" Hare exclaimed. "You horrible creature! How can you throw such dirt on a gentleman with straight ears like me." He took a stone and hurled it at the cock but narrowly missed the target.

One of the king's pregnant wives then came and began to throw more rubbish on Hare. "How, my mother-in law!" Hare exclaimed. "Have you no shame! How can you do that!"

The cock cried out vehemently: "Oh King! Oh King! This visitor of yours here oh King! Is a very, very bad man! Come and chase him away from here!" But the king replied: "Even if he is a bad one, bring him inside."

Hare was taken in and put under the structure. The cock got

on top and began throwing delicious foods down. When a piece of meat fell in front of Hare, he immediately took it and swallowed it whole. The cock looked at him reproachfully, then pushed down a meatless jawbone. "What am I supposed to do with this," he complained. "Throw me boneless meat and honey, do you hear?"

But the cock cried out again: "Oh King! This visitor of yours here is a very, very bad man! Come and throw him out of here!" But the king replied: "Even if he is a bad man, bring him here to me."

The following day Hare was given a gourd full of seeds to sow in the farm. He ate most of the seeds on the way and before midday he returned with the empty gourd.

"What!" the king exclaimed. "Have you finished sowing the seeds so soon? I do not believe you. It will take ten men to finish sowing that amount of seed in such a short time!"

But Hare said: "That is because the men you have here are lazy. In my country we are a very hard working people. If I start working with your men at the same time, I will leave them a long way behind me!"

"That may be so," the king replied, "but I want you to go back and pick up all the seeds and bring them to me. Then I will believe you."

Hare went and called hundreds of doves and weaver birds to help him pick up the seeds. "Friends," he told them, " I have never found an unjust king like this. You all know how difficult it is to pick out every single seed from the ground especially when we are all hungry. So if a seed goes a little deeper in your mouth, you may swallow it up." Both he and the birds ate most of the seeds they found and Hare brought back only a handful. But the king told him: "Go and sow that in the farm again."

Three months later, Hare asked the king to let him return to his own country. The king immediately agreed and gave him many cows and bulls. He was very pleased because he did not expect the king to be so kind. He had hoped to get only two or three old cows, but the king gave him more than a hundred.

When he was half way, however, he noticed that some of the

animals behaved in a strange and wild way. Then one by one they began to change into leopards, hyenas, lions and other fierce animals. But Hare did not mind. He was resolved to bring them home whatever they changed into. But then once again one by one the wild animals began to go away. When he saw one go, he shouted: "Where are you going, you! Come back. This way straight home!" Then the animal would stop and look at Hare menacingly. Immediately, he would say again: "What uncle! I was not speaking to you. I say you can go wherever you like!"

Most of Hare's cattle turned wild and he came home only with six old cows, which he kept tied on tethers around his house.

Loo'boo and His Mother

Once upon a time, there was an old woman who had no children. She lived all by herself. She had many cattle, goats and sheep, but nobody in the village respected her because she was barren. The other women told their children never to go near her home or accept anything from her. When she went to fetch water at the well, the other women always made her wait until they filled their pots first.

"We have left our children starving at home. You must wait until we have filled our pots," they would say. "After all you have no child to look after." The old woman put up with these insults for years. She was very sad but never complained. But as time went by, she found that she could not look after her increasing cattle, goats, sheep and chicken. Often she had to work from early morning until late at night. When the dry season came and there was no fresh grass near her home, she had to take her cattle to the distant hills for fresh pasture. At times she did not return until it was very late at night.

So the old woman decided to make a last effort to get a child. She took one white cock and one black cock and sacrificed them at the sacred grove of her ancestors. She pleaded with them to bless her with a child to look after her cattle. This time her prayers were answered and she became pregnant.

At first the people thought she was ill when they noticed her extending stomach, because no woman at her age ever had a child. But other women, who were experts in child birth, declared that it was an ordinary pregnancy and not a disease.

It soon became clear that the old woman's baby was not an ordinary child. He grew so quickly inside his mother that within one month he was ready to be born. He kicked about against the walls of his mother's womb and often made it impossible for her to work. But this time some of the people were no longer unkind to the old woman, since now she too was going to have a baby. So they looked after her cattle.

At the end of the second month the old woman's stomach was so large that she could not get up. She spent all her time sitting under one of her granaries. Then one afternoon as she was sitting there, she heard her baby speak to her from inside her womb:

Mother, I am coming
Mother, I am coming
Get some arrows and a bow ready for me!

The old woman was very shocked, but said nothing about it to anybody. She knew people would not believe her, instead they would think she was mad. Besides she had grown to accept that her child was not an ordinary one. So she got the arrows and a bow and put them in the house.

And the very next morning the old woman gave birth to a strongly-built baby boy. His hair was rough and thick like that of an adult's. He also had all his teeth, full and strong. Moreover, he could talk properly and seemed to know all his mother's troubles without her explaining them to him. The old woman called him Loo'boo.

The next morning, before the old woman woke up, Loo'boo took all the goats and sheep in the compound and tethered them in the bushes around their home. Then after breakfast he took his arrows and bow and said he was going to take the cattle out to graze.

"You stay here, Loo'boo, my child," the old woman begged. "You were only born yesterday. You are too young to look after cattle. Do not go. I will look after the cattle myself, my son!"

But Loo'boo would not listen. He took a gourd of water with him and drove the cattle to the distant hills. It was a place the other people were too afraid to go. There were many wild animals there, like hyenas, leopards and lions. But Loo'boo shot these animals dead with his arrows when they attacked his cattle, and brought all the cattle home without a single one missing.

The old woman became very proud of Loo'boo. So the next morning when he took the cattle out to graze, his mother did not try to stop him. She gave him a gourd of water and some food and told him to go well.

Soon, the old woman became the envy of everyone in the village. None of the other boys or men worked as hard or efficiently as Loo'boo. His mother's cattle became the fattest and the healthiest in the whole kingdom, because he always took them to the best grass. All the women began to advise their children and even husbands to follow Loo'boo's example. All the girls in the surrounding areas fondly longed for him, secretly wishing that Loo'boo would one day become their husband. Now, when the old woman went to fetch water at the well, all the other women made her fill her pot first. She was treated like the chief's wife.

One day Loo'boo took the cattle even farther than before. And finding the grass there even more green and lush, he decided to make a temporary camp there, intending to return when the cattle finished the grass. He did not return home after five days and his mother was heartbroken. She went about asking everyone if they had seen or heard of Loo'boo. Everyone told her they had not. She returned home and refused to eat or drink water. A week passed, but Loo'boo did not come back. The old woman nearly went insane because of worry.

So on the seventh day she set out following the way Loo'boo took the cattle. After travelling for a long time she became too tired to move and sat down on a small hill and began to sing:

Loo'boo we wee Loo'boo
Loo'boo ca tini kuru Loo'boo
Loo'boo yo ma ng'wa'api Loo'boo
Loo'boo ica tini kuru Loo'boo!

(Loo'boo oh Loo'boo
Loo'boo you are too young for the cattle, Loo'boo
Loo'boo my beloved son Loo'boo
You are not old enough for the cattle Loo'boo).

She sang her song day and night. Everyone who heard her

sad voice felt sorry for her. In the end someone went to look for Loo'boo, and when he was told that his mother was dying of worry, he immediately drove the cattle back. After this Loo'boo promised not to go away from home again. And the old woman spent the rest of her days in complete happiness. Who would not? After all, she was the mother of a son anyone could be proud of.

Pereni-Denge and The Jealous Sisters

A long time ago there lived a handsome young man called Pereni-Denge. He was so handsome that all the women in the kingdom wanted to become his wife. However, Pereni-Denge refused all of them. He refused to marry even the most beautiful women. Whenever someone said: "Pereni-Denge, please marry this or that woman," he would say no. But he did not give any reasons for his strange behaviour.

In a short time, all the girls in the kingdom began to hate one another. Each thought that the other was Pereni-Denge's favourite and would one day become his wife. The jealousies among the women became too much and the king got to hear about them.

One day the king went to Pereni-Denge and asked him to marry one of the girls in the village. "You may not like any of them," the king said, "but you must take one if only to end their rivalries. The jealousy that now fills the hearts of our women because of you is very frightening."

But Pereni-Denge refused to listen. In the end the king got so tired that he ordered the young man to leave his kingdom.

So Pereni-Denge left and made his home on a small island in the middle of River Nile. There he wanted to stay in peace out of reach of anyone and away from women.

However, in a short time he began to feel lonely because there was nobody to speak to on the island, nobody to see, and nobody to admire him. He soon realised that his good looks were useless since he was alone on the island. So he sent word to the king that he was ready to marry the first woman who could swim to him.

When this was announced, there was a lot of excitement in the kingdom. Everyone was happy that at last Pereni-Denge was going to get married. But this excitement did not last long. Some girls who tried to swim to Pereni-Denge at night all

drowned. Some were eaten by crocodiles and sharks. The king's daughter was one of the ones who died.

The king then decided that the best way to see who could swim to Pereni-Denge was to organise an open competition in broad daylight. On the chosen day all the girls who were interested assembled at the river bank. The king blew the whistle and the girls splashed into the river, each trying to win the man she loved. But the water was flowing so strongly that none got even half-way before returning to the bank.

But there were two sisters called Liia and Olio who did not turn up for the competition. The two were both secret admirers of Pereni-Denge. When they saw that none of the other girls had succeeded, they both came forward. The two also happened to be the most beautiful and strongest of the maidens in the land.

As Liia was the elder, she tried first. She splashed into the river and for a long time completely disappeared under the water. Then she emerged almost half way and everyone thought she would make it to Pereni-Denge. Her powerful arms beat the water as she forged ahead. But just at this moment Olio, who had been cheering her sister excitedly, became worried that she would be beaten. She was a girl of quick decisions, and so shouted loudly to her sister:"LIIA! LIIA MY SISTER! A CROCODILE IS COMING TO CATCH YOU! A CROCODILE IS COMING TOWARDS YOU! COME BACK QUICKLY! A CROCODILE! A CROCODILE!" Liia heard her and quickly turned back. The fear of crocodiles drove her towards the bank even faster than she had swam.

When Liia discovered that she had been cheated she became terribly angry, but there was nothing she could do. It was now Olio's turn.

Olio said goodbye to her mother and father, and jumped into the river with a huge splash. At first she swam very slowly as if she was already tired. When she got about half-way, she disappeared completely under the water and many thought a crocodile had seized her. But just then she emerged far away in the distance and was still splashing at a terrific speed towards the island.

Liia remembered how she had been tricked. She shouted out to Olio: "Olio! Olio my sister. A crocodile is coming to catch you! Come back!"

But Olio swam on as if she had heard nothing. She could already see the top of Pereni-Denge's house and this made her more determined.

Olio reached Pereni-Denge's island safely and the two immediately got married. The king announced that Pereni-Denge and his wife could come to live in the kingdom.

Pereni-Denge and Olio lived happily ever after and they had many children.

Adua and Kenyi

Lion loved eating babies' flesh. His appetite for tender flesh was so strong that it could not be satisfied. His wife bore him twelve children, and he ate all of them. He made it a habit to stay at home whenever his wife had a large stomach so that he could eat the child the moment it was born.

When his wife became pregnant for the thirteenth time, she knew it was her last baby and was determined to save it. She went to Tortoise for help. After the divination, tortoise told her: "You must deliver the baby away from home. When you come back to the house, put it in the family *etee* and keep it in the granary. Feed the baby only when your husband is not at home. Do this until the child can sit and run about. After that Lion will do no harm and will instead become very fond of the child."

Lion's wife did as she was told. She delivered a beautiful baby girl and took care of her as advised by Tortoise. Often Lion would watch his wife and say: "Where is that thing in your stomach? Your belly used to be large, but now it is flat."

But she always replied: "Do not mock me over my misfortune, Lion. You can see I am past the age of child-bearing. What is this you are talking about? Please let me suffer in peace." And she would start crying, and Lion would walk away. This is how the baby was saved.

When she eventually brought the child out of the granary, everyone marvelled at her beauty. Nobody had seen such a beautiful girl before. Her skin was as smooth as oil and her teeth were as white as milk. Lion was very fond of the child and considered himself the most proud father. He gave her the name Adua, which meant "in oil". Lion decreed that Adua must not eat anything except drink milk, and that she must stay at home at all times and do no work. And that was how Adua grew up.

One day Adua's age-mates came to her when both her parents were away and asked her to go with them to the river

to fetch water. But Adua refused. She said: "If I go out the sun will make me melt."

They said: "We will take pots of cold water and as soon as you feel hot we will pour the water on you so you will not melt."

In the end Adua was persuaded to go to the river. Every time she felt hot the girls poured cold water on her, which prevented her from melting.

When they got to the stream they found a young man named Kenyi looking after his cattle. He was struck by Adua's beauty. He asked the girls to take him some water to drink but each time he refused to accept the water. At last Adua took him water in her special cowrie shell emblemished bowl. Kenyi accepted the water and refused to return Adua's bowl. Instead he began to drive his cattle home, to another kingdom. Adua followed him, weeping and singing.

Ka ka ka ka ayakuo ayakuo
Tii mejijo ri'ingo'a?
Meri'a Adua ni'ingo'a?
Gbayi Gbayi ni'ingo'a?
Oju Gbayi ni'ngo'a?
Nyenzi drwi kefee!

(No no no! I am not going.
I will not go.
Where are the cattle for my dowry?
Where is Meri-Adua?
Where is Gbayi Gbayi?
Where is the one with the big horns?
Set them loose and let them come!)

Kenyi would cordon off fifty or so cows each time Adua stopped singing her enchanting song with her lovely voice and sent them running into Lion's kraal. As Kenyi and Adua got closer to his kingdom an endless stream of cattle kept pouring into Lion's home. Adua demanded cattle at every move, before washing her hands, before eating, before everything. And for seven days cattle continued to stream into Lion's compound.

Lion spent all his time running around the huge herd to stop them from straying.

Now Kenyi put Adua in the care of his senior wife. He forbade her from giving Adua anything except milk. He also forbade the use of Adua's special bowl for anything else.

But one day, in her forgetfulness, the senior wife took the special bowl and poured millet porridge in it. When Kenyi returned from herding his cattle, his wife gave him porridge in the special bowl. He was so outraged that he refused to drink it. He ordered his wife to wash every bit of millet from it. After this they tested it more than ten times to see if any particle of millet was left. They poured fresh milk into it, but not a single millet particle appeared. In the end Kenyi was satisfied that the bowl was safe for Adua to use.

But unfortunately, a single millet skin had remained in one of the cowrie shells. It got stuck in Adua's throat when she was drinking the milk and she immediately died from suffocation.

Kenyi was very distressed. He knew Lion would become very angry if he heard of his dear daughter's sudden death. He dared not take the bad news himself. So he collected large amounts of every kind of food and set out to find someone who could bear the message to his in-law.

He found Cow. "How do you sing?" he asked.
"I sing: 'Mooo' ", Cow replied.
"You are not for me".
He found Dog. "How do you sing?"
"I sing: 'Gbooo-Gbooo!'".
"You are not for me."
In the end he found Ram running about in a dry river bed.
"How do you sing?"
"I sing: 'Meeeeeeh....' "
"Please complete your song for me."
"I am hungry."
He gave him some more food. "How do you sing?"
"I sing: 'Meeeeeh, Adua....' "
"Please complete your song for me."
"I am still hungry." In this way Kenyi got Ram to sing his song which ran as follows:

Meeeee - Adua'i yoo
Ebi'a zaan'gwa tidia ni kpwo!
Meeeee - Adua'i yoo
A'awa'a zaan'gwa tidia ni kpwo!

(Meeeeeh, Adua! Meeeeh, Adua!
The king's noble daughter has died;
Lion's noble daughter is dead!)

Kenyi gave the rest of the food to Ram, and said to him: "You are the one I am looking for. Quick, pass on the message to my in-law the Lion." And Ram immediately set out on his long race across the hills.

Lion was at home that day. His wife had died and he lived alone with his cattle. The nearest person to his compound was an old woman who spent most of her time in front of her door. Lion had just finished milking a cow when the old woman came over to him.

"Lion, I hear something like your daughter Adua is dead."

"Woman!" Lion roared. "Why are you wishing such evil on my young daughter? How could you say that a daughter who brought me all these cattle is dead? Why do you not wish death on yourself?" With this he seized the old woman and pushed her head into hot ashes.

But the old woman was convinced she heard the message. "Lion," she said again. "I still hear something like Adua is dead. Just try to listen and you will hear it for yourself." But Lion was too angry now even to answer her. He only gazed at her and wished he could do something that could kill her at a single stroke.

Meantime, Ram drew nearer and nearer, bellowing his message louder and louder.

At last Lion heard it too. Immediately he stopped what he was doing and listened again. Ram's voice was now quite clear.

Meeeeh, Adua! Meeeh, Adua!
The king's noble daughter has died!
Lion's noble daughter is dead!

Lion ran and hid himself at the gate to await Ram's arrival. He wanted to kill him there and then. But Ram knew about this and he jumped over Lion and got into the compound. He ran around the compound three times singing at the top of his voice. Lion ran after him everywhere and the ground shook. Finally Ram jumped out of the compound and headed for the hills.

Lion ran after him. The two ran all the way to Kenyi's kingdom and right into his compound. When they got there Ram escaped through a side gate. Lion began to swallow everything in sight. He swallowed all Kenyi's remaining cattle, granaries and houses. It was only when not a single thing was left in the compound that he stopped to rest.

Kenyi, who had been hiding, came out and begged Lion to calm down. "It was not my fault," he said. "It was the fault of my wife. Please be calm and allow me to bring back your daughter." But Lion said nothing.

Then from under the water pot, Kenyi took the leaves on which he had put Adua's blood. He went to the back of the house and hit it with a stick. It became a python.

"Adua, why do you change into a python for me? Was it I who killed you?" He hit the leaves again and again, until in the end Adua came back to life. He handed her back to her father, who was very pleased and took her back to his kingdom.

Little Chick and Millipede

Little Chick and Millipede were great friends. They lived in the same compound and they were always together.

One day Little Chick asked Millipede to accompany him to a nearby stream for a bath. When they got there they took off their clothes and started bathing. Millipede asked Little Chick to rub his back, because his hands were too short. Little Chick agreed, and after rubbing his friend's back a few times, he said: "My friend, your back is so clean that there is nothing to wash. The water just runs off like dew on banana leaves."

He then asked Millipede to rub his back in return. Millipede splashed some water on Little Chick's feathers, pushed his hands through them and then out again and said: "My friend, your back is so dirty that nobody can wash it. Water cannot go through your feathers. Your back is now so filthy that it stinks.

Little Chick was ashamed because his back was so dirty. He envied his friend. He was also very annoyed that Millipede had told him on the face that his back was smelling. So when Millipede was drying his body in the sun, Little Chick suddenly picked him with his beak and swallowed him.

When he got home, people asked him: "Little Chick, where have you left Millipede?" Little Chick did not say a word.

"Little Chick, where have you left Millipede?" they asked again.

Again, Little Chick did not open his mouth.

"LITTLE CHICK, WHERE HAVE YOU LEFT MILLIPEDE?" they shouted.

At last Little Chick said: "*Mgba-aaa-aa! Mgba-aaa-aaa!*" That is to say:"Here in my belly— here in my belly— here in my belly!"

The people realised what had happened. They grabbed Little Chick, tied his hands and feet tightly with fibres and carried him back to the stream. They slit open his stomach and removed Millipede, who was still alive. They threw Little

Chick's body in the water, which carried it down the adjoining streams, over many big and small falls and into the River Nile. They washed Millipede clean and took him home.

Liia and Her Suitors

There was an old woman who had only one daughter called Liia. She was the daughter of a spirit, because her mother only conceived after many divinations and offering of sacrifices.

Liia grew up very quickly and became the most beautiful woman in the country. All the animals came to court her, each bringing a lot of gifts. But Liia's mother did not allow any of the suitors to talk to her daughter.

"You see I am an old woman now," she would tell the suitors. "Liia is my arm and leg. I cannot live without her. You will marry her only after you have done whatever I ask you, not before." So whenever a suitor arrived, Liia would tell him to talk to her mother first.

Hare was among the earliest suitors. He put on his new clothes and combed his hair in a style nobody had ever seen before. After the customary greetings, he went straight to the old woman and asked for her daughter's hand in marriage.

"Young man," the old woman said, "I do not want any bride price. But if you want to marry Liia, you must do two things. First, you must stamp your feet in front of my house until you make a well. When Liia is away, I will get my water right here. I am old and cannot go to the river."

Then, you must climb up the big *eleu* tree behind the house and shake the branches to bring all the fruits down, so I can live on them for the rest of my days," she continued.

Hare agreed to do both things at once. He took off his shirt and began to stamp his feet on the hard ground near the old woman's door. But he only succeeded in raising dust. He gave up on this and went to climb the tree. Again he failed, because the tree was very tall and so thick that his hands could not go around it. The following day, he came with his brothers and friends to assist him, but they too failed.

Soon word of what the old woman was asking for her

29

daughter spread across the country. Suitors from near and far came to the compound in large numbers. For weeks and months the animals tried their best to perform the tasks but none succeeded. Even large animals like Lion, Hippopotamus, Rhino and Buffalo failed.

In the end, Elephant, who had shown little interest in Liia now suddenly became interested when it seemed nobody else could marry her. One day he arrived at the old woman's compound with great flourish. He had had an early bath in the river and the skin on his back shone in the morning sun. All the animals who had been defeated by the feat came to watch him.

Elephant started with the well. The whole earth shook as he furiously stamped the ground. But instead of water, Elephant turned the whole compound into a pool of dust which rose in the air like smoke. Next he went to the *eleu* tree. In his rage, he attempted to uproot it, but could not. He tried to knock the fruits down with sticks, but only a few fell.

At this stage the suitors began to talk excitedly among themselves. They complained that the old woman's tasks were impossible. Leopard even suggested in whispers that they should kill the obstinate woman and carry Liia away by force. Their plan was popular at first, but was not carried out.

It was at this stage that Chameleon, who nobody had thought about, arrived unobserved and announced that he wanted Liia for his wife.

II

Chameleon's appearance was greeted with indignant uproar and scoffs from other suitors. "What a shame!" someone exclaimed. "Do you really think you have the smallest chance when the strongest of us have failed?"

Another ventured: "Chameleon, go home. You may be able to change your colours, but this is not the same thing!"

"Ha ha ha!" yet another laughed.

But Chameleon ignored them and walked in a dignified manner to where Liia was sitting and formally proposed to her. This confidence enraged the other animals. They threw things at him. But Liia told Chameleon to talk to her mother.

In a short while, Chameleon was in the dust in front of the house. The rest of the suitors surrounded him. The animals were still jeering at him for daring to show his face. But instead Chameleon broke into a song as he danced on the ground with his feet.

Molu Lindre'i rii-
Ma vu di tu e'yii!
Molu Kaa'i riii-
Ma vu di tu e'yii!
Molu Opi'i rii-
Vu di kega e'yii!

(If I am Chameleon
I will make a well here!
If I am the son of kaa
I will make a well here!
If I am the King
This ground will become water!)

Chameleon sang in such a lovely voice that the other animals found themselves nodding their heads and moving their feet in rhythm. They were so carried away by the song that in fact they did not notice the first streaks of water that appeared under Chameleon's feet. The dust had turned moist and Chameleon had changed his colour to grey. The animals were dumbfounded. They were angry and envious as it became clear that Chameleon was going to succeed.

Chameleon was now singing at the top of his voice. His voice rang of a magic spell. There was power, vehemence, longing and love in his voice. All the animals were afraid of him now. Everything was quiet save for Chameleon's powerful voice.

In time, water appeared. It was so pure and clear that the animals saw their noses in it. Chameleon worked on until he was completely covered with water, then continued to work under it. It was only when the whole compound was covered by the well that he came out.

The animals refused to talk to him now. They all rushed to the tree to prevent him from climbing. But Liia's mother personally carried Chameleon in the family *etee* to the foot of the *eleu* tree. She chased the jealous animals away, and told Chameleon to climb the tree. Chameleon looked around, without turning his head, and began to climb the *eleu* tree.

He was slow and counted three times before taking each limb forward. This time he sang a different song.

> *Hwe ma'a tule ri'i nyi tua wa yaa?*
> *Kiido kodoo*
> *Hwee ma tule ri'i nyi tua wa yaa?*
> *Kiido kodoo!*
> *Hwe matulerii nyitua wa'ya?*
> *Lindre, kodoo!*

The animals anxiously watched as he slowly made his way up the tree. But several of the more bad tempered ones threatened to kill him if he did not come down at once. But Chameleon ignored the threats. When he was above the reach of most of the animals, Elephant suddenly shot up his long trunk and violently pulled Chameleon down. There was loud applause.

Now Chameleon pretended to be dead. The animals started celebrating and soon forgot all about Chameleon. He had changed his colour so that none of the other animals could see him.

He climbed the *eleu* tree silently. The next thing that happened was the fruits from the tree were falling like hailstorm. Chameleon shook every branch with such force that all the fruits fell. He went from branch to branch again to make sure that not a single fruit was left.

Chameleon's success and the realisation that he was now the husband of the most beautiful woman in the country filled the other animals with rage as they left the old woman's homestead. They could not bear to see such an ugly creature like Chameleon actually taking the beautiful Liia to his home.

When Chameleon came down, the old woman put him in the *etee* again and carried him to her house. There he feasted on the most delicious foods and rested until the following day. And by sunrise, Liia and Chameleon were heading for their new home, as man and wife. And because her husband walked slowly, Liia carried him in her arms, like a child. He told her which way to go.

III

It was the custom that once a woman was married, all her former suitors should leave her alone. They should speak to her normally and respect her new status in life. But a few of Liia's former suitors — Elephant, Leopard, Lion, Hare — found it hard to forget her. They met in secret and planned how to punish and take Chameleon's wife away.

Months went by. The dry season was now over. The rains came and men opened new fields and began digging them to plant millet and *simsim*. Chameleon, now that he was married, worked very hard. His farm was on a large flat plain that could be seen from far off.

But everyday, when the sun was up and women had taken food to their husbands in the fields, the conspirators gathered at one place and looked at Chameleon's farm. The sight of Liia working so energetically beside her husband made them angry. Chameleon knew that these people wanted to kill him and had made preparations to save his life.

One afternoon, he and his wife saw Elephant leading his friends towards their farm. He nodded to his wife and Liia quickly took him and put him in the family *etee*, which she placed under the shed of a small *melemele* tree.

Elephant and his friends arrived, but Chameleon was nowhere to be seen. He asked Liia where her husband was. "My husband has gone to the river to get some fibres to mend the roof of our granary," she replied.

Elephant and his friends immediately hurried down the river to look for Chameleon. After they left Chameleon came out of his hiding place. Liia quickly gathered a small bundle of firewood and they left the farm for their home.

Liia used this trick to save her husband's life many times. Sometimes she would tell Elephant that Chameleon had gone on a long journey, or that he was having a bath in the nearby stream. Other times she said he was at a meeting of the elders or he had gone hunting. But Elephant now suspected that Liia was fooling him.

So one day they went to look for Tortoise, the seer and diviner. They found him just returning home from the bush, with herbs tied to his back.

"Tortoise! Tortoise!" Elephant screamed at him. "You know that I have all these troubles and now you suddenly appear in front of me. Next time you will force somebody to trample on you."

"Uncle Elephant," Tortoise answered. "Why do you attack me so viciously? What have I done to you? Please do not be angry with me. Let me find out the source of your troubles."

"The most beautiful woman in the world, worthy to be the wife of a king, is married to Chameleon," he explained. "We want to kill him for that. But everyday we go to his farm we cannot find him. I want you to tell me where I can find Chameleon."

"Elephant," Tortoise answered. "How is it that you come to me with such a simple problem? This is one of the things that even a child can solve. But I will help you. If you go there tomorrow, look for Chameleon in the garden and you will find him hidden in the family *etee*, under the small *melemele* tree in the middle of the farm."

Elephant thanked Tortoise and the animals hurried home. They were full of hope, joy and excitement.

The following day Elephant and his friends were at Chameleon's farm earlier than usual. After the customary greetings, they asked Liia where her husband was. "My husband...." Liia began, but Elephant interrupted. "Liia, do you really think we do not know where Chameleon is? Just watch me. I will get him this very minute!" He walked over to the *melemele* tree, and sure enough found Chameleon in the *etee*.

Without wasting time he trampled on him until he died. The other animals jumped on the corpse after Elephant and buried Chameleon under the ground. They went home singing songs of joy, while Liia ran home weeping.

IV

Liia was already pregnant when the jealous animals murdered her husband. She gave birth to a beautiful and stout-limbed baby boy. The boy grew up quickly and everyone agreed that he was not an ordinary child because of his strength and bravery.

It was the custom that children be trained in the art of marksmanship. There was a large arena in the middle of the village for this. Everyday the children, armed with their bows and arrows, trooped to the arena to practice shooting. They stood in one long line on one side of the arena, and someone rolled a large ball of banana fibres down the line in front of them. When a child hit the ball with his arrow, he immediately cried out his *laza*, such as: "By my father the Lion." Those who missed said nothing.

Liia's son did not know his father's name. So when he hit the ball, he shouted: "By my mother! By my mother!" The other children roared with laughter and called him a woman's son and ridiculed him. So one day he asked his mother for his father's name. But Liia told him: "You are still too young to know your father. I will tell you who your father is when you grow up." The boy was therefore teased by his age-mates year after year.

A few years later, when he was older, Liia told him his father's name. She said: "When you hit the ball with your arrow, you should shout as follows: "By my father Chameleon, whom the clan of Elephant, the clan of Lion, the clan of Leopard and the clan of Hare murdered out of envy!"

The boy was excited. He undid his bow and did it again and again. He sharpened his arrows as he had never done before. When at last he was satisfied, he dressed like a warrior and went to the arena. He stood at the farthest end of the line so that he would shoot last. He trembled with excitement as the ball came rolling his way, and paid no attention to the echoes of the other children's victorious cries.

He aimed and shot. No sooner had the arrow buried itself into the ball than he raised his bow and arrows up and cried out bitterly: "By my father Chameleon, whom the clan of Elephant, the clan of Lion, the clan of Leopard and the clan of Hare killed out of envy! By my father Chameleon! By my father Chameleon!"

There was dead silence in the arena. The other boys were frightened. They all turned and fled in terror. Nobody dared look behind. The boy also turned and walked home.

V

Hare knew at once that a terrible retribution would follow now that the boy knew his father and how he had died. He therefore set out to make friends with Chameleon's son without delay. And once the two became friends, Hare became the chief conspirator as they plotted the destruction of those who had murdered Chameleon.

"My son," Hare said to Chameleon's son one day. "You know it is the custom of our people that when someone dies, those left behind must organise a large dance in his honour. We will be destroyed if we do not follow this custom. Your father was a great man. We must now organise a dance suitable for his honour. We will call all the people in the country to attend."

After six months, the organisation for the dance was finished. It was now the dry season and nobody went to work in the fields. So on the day of the dance, people came from all over the country and beyond.

The site of the dance was very far away from any home. It was right in the middle of the wilderness. Hare made sure that the grass in the place was not cleared, but merely trampled on. The drums echoed in the valley and dancers arrived with jingle bells on their feet. The great dance began.

Hare and Chameleon's son at this stage slipped away from the dance in the night. They walked together for some fifty miles and then parted, each going in the opposite direction. They walked in a huge circle around the dance, setting fire to the dry grass as they went. At midnight they met at the other end and both returned to the dance. They found Squirrel and ordered him to make a large and deep hole under a nearby *maza* tree without delay.

Back to the dance, Hare announced it was time for the main song to be sang. This was the song composed by the son of the departed man, to give honour to his father. After Chameleon's son said the words and set the tune, the whole arena had the song by heart within minutes. Everyone liked the song. The Lion, Frog, Bat, Elephant, everyone, all sang happily.

A' awa tia Lindre ni lijo sanga
Nyeye oguu'ga, nyeye acikaa!
Ebi ti Lindre ni lijo saanga
Nyeye oguu'ga, nyeye acikaa!
Lea tia Lindre ni lijo saanga
Nyeye oguu'ga, nyeye acikaa!

(The Lions have murdered Chameleon
Look behind you
And you will see smoke!!
The Elephants have killed Chameleon
Just look behind you
And you will see smoke!!)

The drumbeat throbbed. Eagle was in charge of the mother drum while Scorpion had the smallest drum and Snake the medium sized one. Mothers abandoned their children and joined the dance. The magic words of the song had gone to their heads. And when they looked behind them, there was indeed smoke. So they danced on, like people possessed.

Hyena's wife saw the smoke and thought it was already daylight. So she began to sing her husband's praises:

Nye'ya'a Mio'raa,
Nye'ya'a Mio'raa,
Buzele ke'eya naa!
Nye'ya Moi'raa,
Nye'ya Moi'raa,
Buzele ke'eya naa, buzele ke'eya naa!!

But slowly the fire crept nearer and nearer. By the time the exhausted dancers realised the danger, there was nothing they could do. The fire was all around them. There was no escape. Within a short time the fire engulfed them and they all died, except Hare, Chameleon's son and their families. They had hidden in the hole Squirrel had made under the nearby *maza* tree.

The Two Brothers

Once upon a time there were two brothers who lived together. They had the same father and the same mother. The elder was married with small children, while the younger was not married. The relation between them was not always good and they quarrelled over the most trivial things.

One day while the elder brother was away at his farm an elephant came to the garden of the younger brother and started destroying his field of millet. Without waiting, the younger brother took his brother's spear, which was placed against a granary outside, and threw it at the elephant. The elephant took to flight and ran away, carrying the spear with it.

When the elder brother returned, he was annoyed to find that his spear had been carried away by the elephant.

"Were you out of your mind?" he exclaimed. "How could you throw a spear at an elephant and not know it would take it away? You must go and bring my spear back."

The younger brother went to his house and brought all his spears out. "Here," he said, "take any of my spears and keep it."

But the elder brother refused. "I want my very same spear. Even if you offer me twenty or one hundred spears, I will not take them. I want back the VERY SAME SPEAR." The young brother pleaded with him, but it was of no use. The clan elders also talked to the elder brother, and begged him to take another spear instead, but he refused.

Eventually, the younger brother could no longer bear it and said to his brother: "Alright. I am going to try and find your spear. But if anything happens to me on the way, if I die in the wilderness, my curse will fall upon you and your offspring." He took his spear and left the village to follow the wounded elephant.

He wandered in the wilderness for many weeks, but he

could not find the elephant. He got very hungry and began to eat wild roots and fruits. His hair and beard grew so long that he looked like a wild man. But he did not give up the hunt for the lost spear.

One day, he spotted the elephant still carrying the spear on its side. He followed it. He camped whenever the elephant rested and followed it when it moved on. After three months, the spear fell off the elephant and the younger brother picked it up and returned home.

Nobody could recognise him when he returned to the village because he had grown a long beard, and his hair was so long that it covered his face. He went straight to his elder brother and threw the spear in front of him. "There, take back your spear," he said and went to his house.

Another three months passed by. The younger brother was one day sorting his beads in preparation for a dance. As he was working, the six-year-old daughter of his elder brother came and sat near him. The girl suddenly took a bead and swallowed it.

"Give back my bead!" her uncle demanded. But the little girl only giggled. "Give back my bead!" he repeated. But the child only made faces at him and run back to her father. The uncle followed her, and said to the father: "Your daughter has swallowed one of my beads, and I want it back."

"We cannot get it out," the father said. "You see she has swallowed it. Perhaps we can wait until it comes out."

But the younger brother insisted that he wanted the bead there and then. He refused all offers of other beads. And while they were still arguing, he suddenly took a hunting knife and cut open the child's stomach, extracted his bead and wiped it clean.

"Now I have got back my bead, and have no more problem with you," he said, and went back to his work.

When the elder brother saw his daughter was dead, he took his spear and charged at his brother, intending to kill him there and then. The younger brother ran for his life. His brother chased him, but the younger brother was quicker and soon left him far behind.

After some time, he got to another clan where in one compound he found a group of men thatching a granary which was still on the ground. After the younger brother explained the situation he was in, they asked him to get inside the roof of the granary, which was already well thatched with grass. He got inside and was completely hidden. Meanwhile the men went on with their work as if nothing had happened.

Just then the elder brother arrived, panting carrying his spear. "Have you seen my brother?" he asked.

The wise elders, who knew of the feud between the two brothers, told him they had not seen him. When he was about to leave, the men asked him to assist them lift the roof onto the granary, which was already on poles nearby. As they lifted the roof, the men deftly tilted the lower side to the elder brother. The younger brother in the meantime clung to the wooden framework of the roof and was thus carried aloft with the roof and lowered onto the granary.

The elder brother was satisfied that his enemy was not there and went to look for him elsewhere. Thus the younger brother's life was saved.

The Foolish Woman and Her Wonderful Baby

Once upon a time, a foolish woman was married in a village in Goopi. The people of the village did not like her. She was dull and did not understand even simple riddles. Her husband was advised to marry someone else but he refused. "A young wife needs support, not criticism," he argued. It was impossible to make him see that his wife was so stupid that she would never learn anything.

One year later the foolish woman gave birth to a beautiful baby boy. The people's feelings towards her changed at once. Now that she was a mother of a baby boy her other faults were forgiven. For the woman whose first child was a boy was highly respected.

One day the foolish woman's sister-in-law came to see the baby. She was so enchanted by the baby that she stayed for a long time. It was only when the sun was setting that she rose to go.

"This child of yours is truly lovely," she said. "He has kept me laughing all the time and now my sides ache. Take good care of him. *Nyiba kolu baani leffu teja*. (Let him be for us to wait for *leffu*)."

Now the foolish woman had been unhappy at the way she had been criticised earlier in her marriage. Do not imagine that it never hurt her when she was told over and over again that she did not understand any riddles. Now she was determined to prove that she was as clever as anyone. So she carefully noted her sister-in-law's remark that the wonderful baby should be kept for "waiting for *leffu*", and patiently waited for the *leffu* season.

When the rains came after the dry season, the women, like everybody else, prepared for the *leffu* harvest.

At last the day came. The woman got all her things ready and was determined not to go to sleep, lest she wakes up too late. Her husband's *leffu* was far away in the wilderness and he had gone to spend the night there. She was left alone with the wonderful child.

After the other people in the compound had finished telling their stories and retired to bed, the foolish woman quietly slaughtered the baby, cut the flesh into pieces and put everything to cook in a large pot. A little after midnight, the meal was ready and she rushed to invite her sister-in-law.

" I have cooked the baby now," she announced proudly. "Please come to eat while we wait for *leffu*."

"What are you talking about?" the astonished sister-in-law asked.

"I have cooked the baby."

"What?"

"You remember you told me to keep him for *leffu*."

"I did not mean that you should kill him!" the distraught sister-in-law wailed. "Oh! Oh! My son! I did not mean that you should kill him! Oh! Oh! "

She rushed past the astonished foolish woman and raced to her brother's compound. Her screams pierced the still night. The whole village was stirred and everyone came to see what had happened.

The compound was full of bewildered villagers when the sister-in-law arrived. She went straight to her brother's house. And there, still in the pot, was the wonderful child!

The sister-in-law rushed out and this time made straight for the foolish woman and fell upon her. She pounded her with her fists, scratched her with her nails, screaming: "I did not say that you should kill and cook the boy! I did not tell you to kill him! You...you...you...you!!"

The people were shocked beyond words. They did not know what to do. Everyone agreed that the sister-in-law was right in saying that the baby should be for *leffu*. It was only a way of saying that the child was so entertaining that he could keep people awake until dawn, which was the time of *leffu*. But the foolish woman did not understand this saying.

The Fate of The Honest Thief

Once upon a time, two thieves went to steal cattle in a distant land. One of them was an experienced thief and lived by stealing. The other was a young honest man who hated stealing. He went only because he was lazy and did not wish to work.

They arrived at the chosen place just after midnight. The moon was shinning brightly in the sky and the thieves could clearly see their shadows on the ground. They stopped at the gate and listened.

"Let us go in now," the experienced thief said. "The people are still sleeping."

But the honest thief said,"I think I would rather stay here. I do not want to go into other people's compound to steal. When you get the cow we will take it away together."

But the experienced thief said:"Very well. Wait for me here then." He then climbed over the fence into the compound.

The compound had two gates. The houses stood in a circle inside the fence. The cattle kraal was in the centre of the compound, surrounded by the houses. The experienced thief made his way to the kraal and then quietly slipped in. He selected a cow and then quietly left the compound by the opposite gate.

The honest thief waited for a long time, but his friend did not come. He was frightened because the eastern horizon was already becoming pale. The birds in the nearby thicket had also began to sing. Somewhere a cock crowed for the second time. The honest thief became impatient and began to call out to his friend:

> Mozi nye'enji ti kevu eze'ezee
> Bazidri ega male ahwi koo:
> Ghugbule ga ri a'gura
> Buzele ga ri a'gura!

(My friend,
Bring the cow out quickly.
I am not going into other people's compound.
Daylight is now close;
The eastern horizon is now pale.
Uncle, bring the cow quickly!)

His voice tore the still night and woke up the men of the compound. One elder got out and went around conferring with each elder in whispers. In a short time they agreed on a course of action.

Meantime, the honest thief continued calling out to his friend his voice becoming hoarse.

The men of the compound, armed with spears and *pangas*, came on their knees and surrounded the thief. Then at a signal from one of them, they all sprung at the honest thief and seized him by the neck. He was beaten to death.

The Cattle Plague of Lefori

The Madi region of Lefori is best known for its elephants and *ituu*, or palm trees. Metu is known for its hills and cattle, Laropi for its fish and cattle, and Muyo for its cattle and *awa*, that marvellous tree from which oil is made and which at one time the chiefs monopolised. But Lefori is mentioned only when people talk about elephants and *ituu*, or when people talk about the absence of cattle.

It had not always been like this, so they say. There was a time when the region of Lefori had just as many cows as any region in Madi. But then all of a sudden the cattle of Lefori began to die and in a short time not a single cow or bull was left. All attempts to reintroduce cattle to Lefori after that time had failed. All animals taken there died within weeks or even days. Many Madi men married women from Lefori because they never ask for cattle for dowry. As far as cattle are concerned, the region of Lefori is under a permanent curse.

It is said that one morning, the proud Chief Adigesi of Lefori went to inspect his cattle in the kraal just outside the royal palace. It was his first ever visit to the kraal after his enthronement. The servants had thoroughly swept the kraal for the occasion. So when Adigesi arrived not a speck of dirt could be seen, not a single animal drop was about and he was very pleased that his animals were so clean.

But as the Chief was about to return to his palace, a cow just in front of him began to defecate, raising up its tail and stooping a bit. The Chief was outraged at this open disrespect shown to him by the animal.

"Obitsa-aaa!" he swore.

He rushed at the cow, scooped the dung in his hands and at once blocked the animal's bottom. He then said to all around:

"Obitsa-aaa! Do cows defecate at home? Quick, block up their bottoms!"

The servants immediately carried out the Chief's orders. From that day onwards they had orders to ensure that no animal ever defecated at home. And in a short while, one by one, the cows began to die. Within a short time all the cattle in Lefori died and all attempts to reintroduce cattle there ever since have failed. Some wandering travellers had on occasions told the people of Lefori that their cattle had died from the bite of some insects called tsetse fly, but of course the people of Lefori knew better.

To this day the people of Lefori only see cattle when they go to visit distant places, or when the animals are taken along the road from Muyo to Lugbara.